Paddington
and the
Marmalade
Maze

First published as a hardback in Great Britain by HarperCollins Publishers in 1987
First published as a paperback edition by Collins Picture Lions in 2001
The edition published by HarperCollins Children's Books in 2009

3 5 7 9 10 8 6 4 2 1

ISBN-13: 978-0-00-786520-8

HarperCollins Children's Books is a division of HarperCollins Publishers Ltd.

Text copyright © Michael Bond 1987
Illustrations copyright © R.W. Alley 1999

Visit our website at: www.harpercollins.co.uk
Printed and bound in Thailand

MICHAEL BOND

Paddington
and the
Marmalade
Maze

illustrated by R.W. ALLEY

HarperCollins *Children's Books*

One day, Paddington's friend, Mr Gruber, took him on an outing to a place called Hampton Court Palace.

"I think you will enjoy it, Mr Brown," he said as they drew near. "It's very old and it has over one thousand rooms. Lots of Kings and Queens have lived here."

Paddington always enjoyed his outings with
Mr Gruber and he couldn't wait to see inside
the Palace.

As they made their way through an arch, Mr Gruber pointed to a large clock.

"That's a very special clock," he said. "It not only shows the time, it tells you what month it is."

"Perhaps we should hurry, Mr Gruber," said Paddington anxiously. "It's half past June already."

They hadn't been inside the Palace very long before they came across a room which had the biggest bed Paddington had ever seen.

"Queen Anne used to sleep in it," said Mr Gruber.

"I expect they put the rope round it to stop her falling out when she had visitors," said Paddington, looking at all the people.

"This is known as the 'Haunted Gallery'," said Mr Gruber. "They do say that when Catherine Howard's ghost passes by you can feel a cold draught."

Paddington shivered. "I hope she's got a duffle coat like mine!" he said.

Mr Gruber took Paddington to see the kitchen next.

"In the old days they used wood fires," he explained. "That's why there is such a high ceiling. There was a lot of smoke."

"I was hoping they might have left some Royal buns behind," said Paddington, licking his lips.

"Talking of buns," said Mr Gruber, "I think it's time we had our lunch."

He led the way outside and they sat down together on the edge of a pool.

As Paddington opened his suitcase he accidentally dropped one of his sandwiches into the water. It was soon alive with goldfish.

"They must like marmalade," said Mr Gruber. "I wonder if that's how they got their name?"

When they had finished their sandwiches, Mr Gruber took Paddington to see 'The Great Vine'.

"It's very famous," he said. "Every year they pick over five hundred bunches of grapes. Imagine that, Mr Brown!"

"I'm trying to, Mr Gruber," said Paddington. "I think I might plant a grape pip when I get back home."

Mr Gruber chuckled. "I'm afraid you will have a long wait, Mr Brown," he said. "That vine is over two hundred years old."

"Now," said Mr Gruber, "before we leave we must visit the famous maze. Sometimes it takes people hours to find their way out."

"I hope that doesn't happen to us," said Paddington. "My paws are getting tired."

"Perhaps it's time I took you home," said Mr Gruber.

Much to his surprise, the words were no sooner out of his mouth than everyone around them began to talk.

"Hey, that sounds a great idea," said a man in a striped shirt.

"Please to wait while I buy a new film for my camera," said a Japanese lady.

"I've never been inside a real English home before," said another lady. "I wonder if they serve tea?

"Oh, dear!" whispered Mr Gruber. "They must think I'm one of the guides. What shall we do?"

"Mrs Bird won't be very pleased if they all follow us home," exclaimed Paddington. "She only has a small teapot."

Then he had an idea.

"Follow me," he called. "I think perhaps we ought to go in the maze after all."

"Are you sure we are doing the right thing?" gasped Mr Gruber, as he hurried on behind.

"Bears are good at mazes," said Paddington. "You need to be in Darkest Peru. The forests are very thick."

And sure enough, before Mr Gruber had time to say any more, Paddington led the way out, leaving everyone else inside.

"How ever did you manage to do that,
Mr Brown?" gasped Mr Gruber.

"Quickest visit I've ever seen," agreed the
man in the ticket office.

"I used marmalade chunks to show where
we had been," said Paddington. "It's something
my Aunt Lucy taught me before she went into
the Home For Retired Bears."

"But I thought you had eaten all your sandwiches," said Mr Gruber.

"I always keep a spare one under my hat in case I have an emergency," said Paddington. "That's something else Aunt Lucy taught me. She'll be very pleased when she hears."

And he stopped at a kiosk to buy a picture postcard so that he could write and tell her all about his day out.

POSTCARDS

That night when he went to bed, as well as the postcard and a pen, Paddington took some rope.

"It's something Queen Anne used to do," he announced. "I've a lot to tell Aunt Lucy and I don't want to fall out of bed before I've finished."